Sally Morgan & Johnny Warrkatja Malibirr

the river

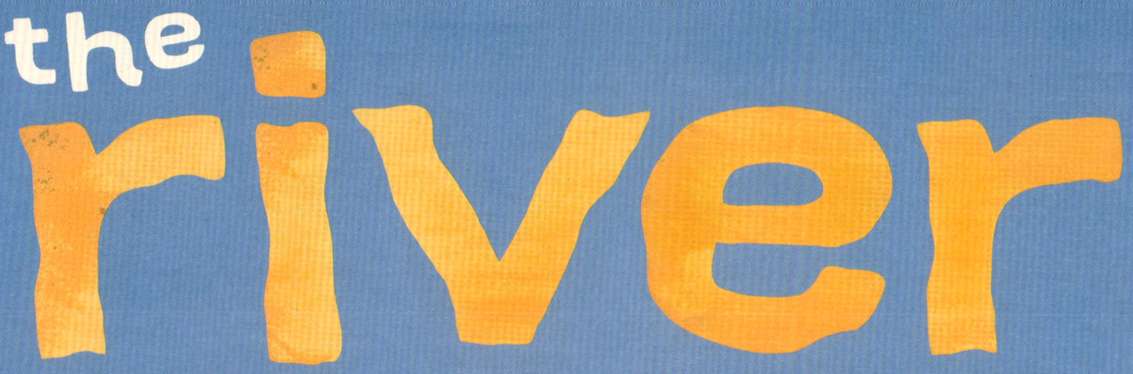

Magabala Books

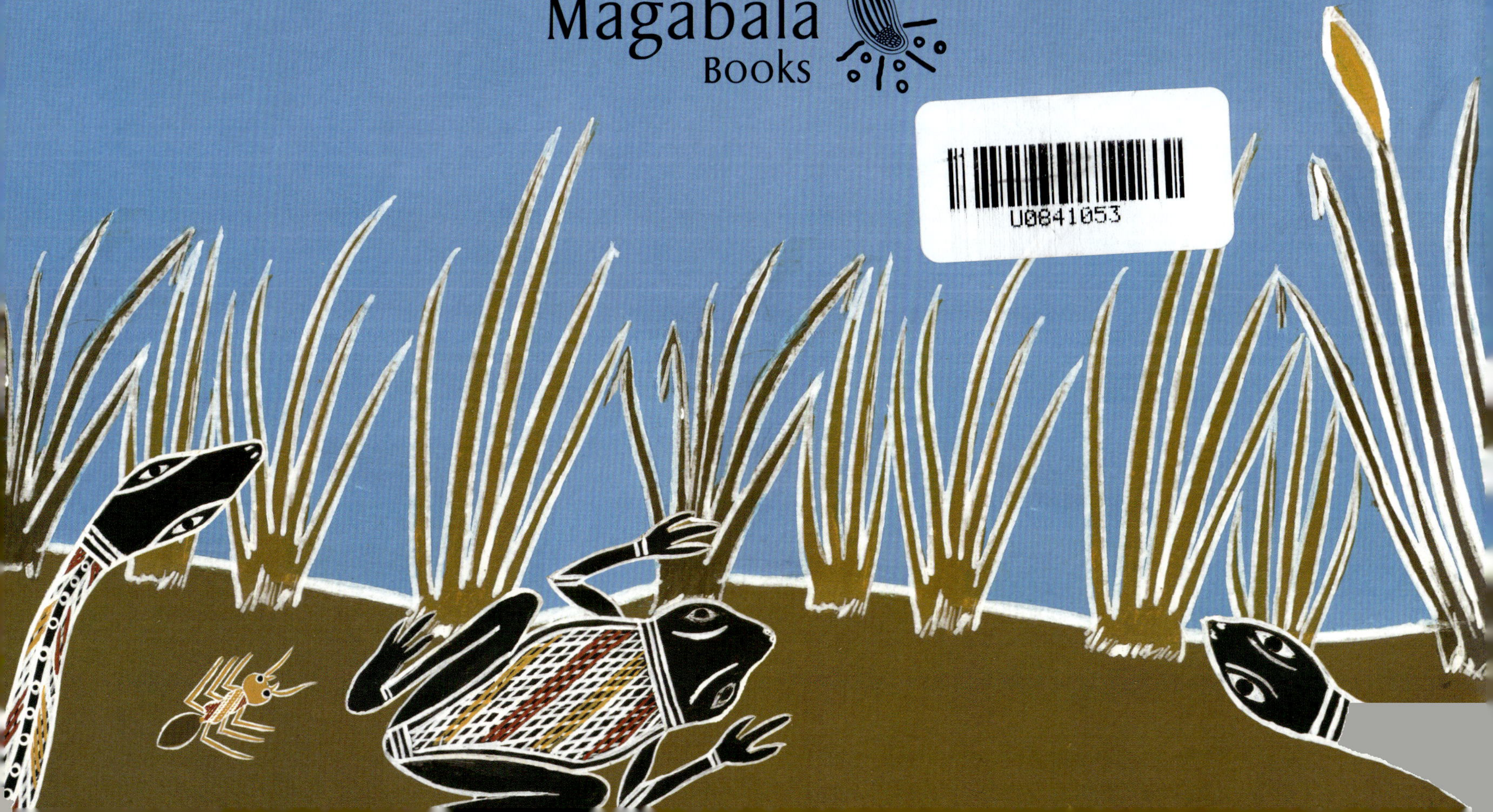

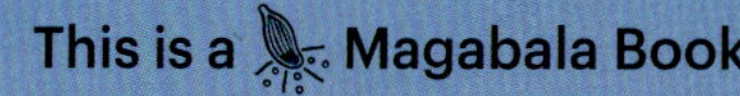

This is a Magabala Book

Leading Publisher of Aboriginal and
Torres Strait Islander Storytellers.

Changing the World, One Story at a Time.

First published 2021. Reprinted 2022, 2023, 2026
Magabala Books Aboriginal Corporation
1 Bagot Street, Broome, Western Australia
Website: www.magabala.com
Email: sales@magabala.com

Magabala Books is assisted by the Australian Government through Creative Australia, its principal arts investment and advisory body, and publishes with support from the WA Government.

Magabala Books is Australia's leading independent Aboriginal and Torres Strait Islander publishing house. We acknowledge the Traditional Owners of the Country on which we live and work. We recognise the unbroken connection to traditional lands, waters and cultures. Through what we publish, we honour all our Elders, peoples and stories, past, present and future.

Designed by Emilia Toia
Printed and bound in China by Everbest Printing Company

ISBN 978-1-922613-02-8 (print)
ISBN 978-1-922613-03-5 (ePDF)

A catalogue record for this book is available from the National Library of Australia

the river

For my grandmother

SM

To my mum Lucy Wanapuyngu

JWM

I love the river near my home.

I look with my eyes,

I listen with my ears,

I learn about the life of the river.

Look with your eyes,

what do you see?

I see green ants,
CRAWL, CRAWL, CRAWLING
over the leaves in the trees.

Listen with your ears,
what do you **hear**?

I hear a **frog**,

CROAK, CROAK, CROAKING

amongst the river reeds.

Look with your eyes,

what do you **see**?

I see a **goanna**,

RUN, RUN, RUNNING

along the soft river bank.

Listen with your ears,
what do you **hear**?

I hear a **fish**,

SPLASH, SPLASH, SPLASHING

in the cool river water.

Look with your eyes,
what do you **see**?

I see a **turtle**,

PEEP, PEEP, PEEPING

from the thick river grass.

Listen with your ears,

what do you **hear**?

I hear an **emu**,

CALL, CALL, CALLING

between the tall river trees.

Look with your eyes,

what do you see?

I see a kangaroo,

JUMP, JUMP, JUMPING

among the low river bushes.

Listen with your ears,
what do you **hear**?

I hear a **goose**,

SCRATCH, SCRATCH, SCRATCHING

in the murky river mud.

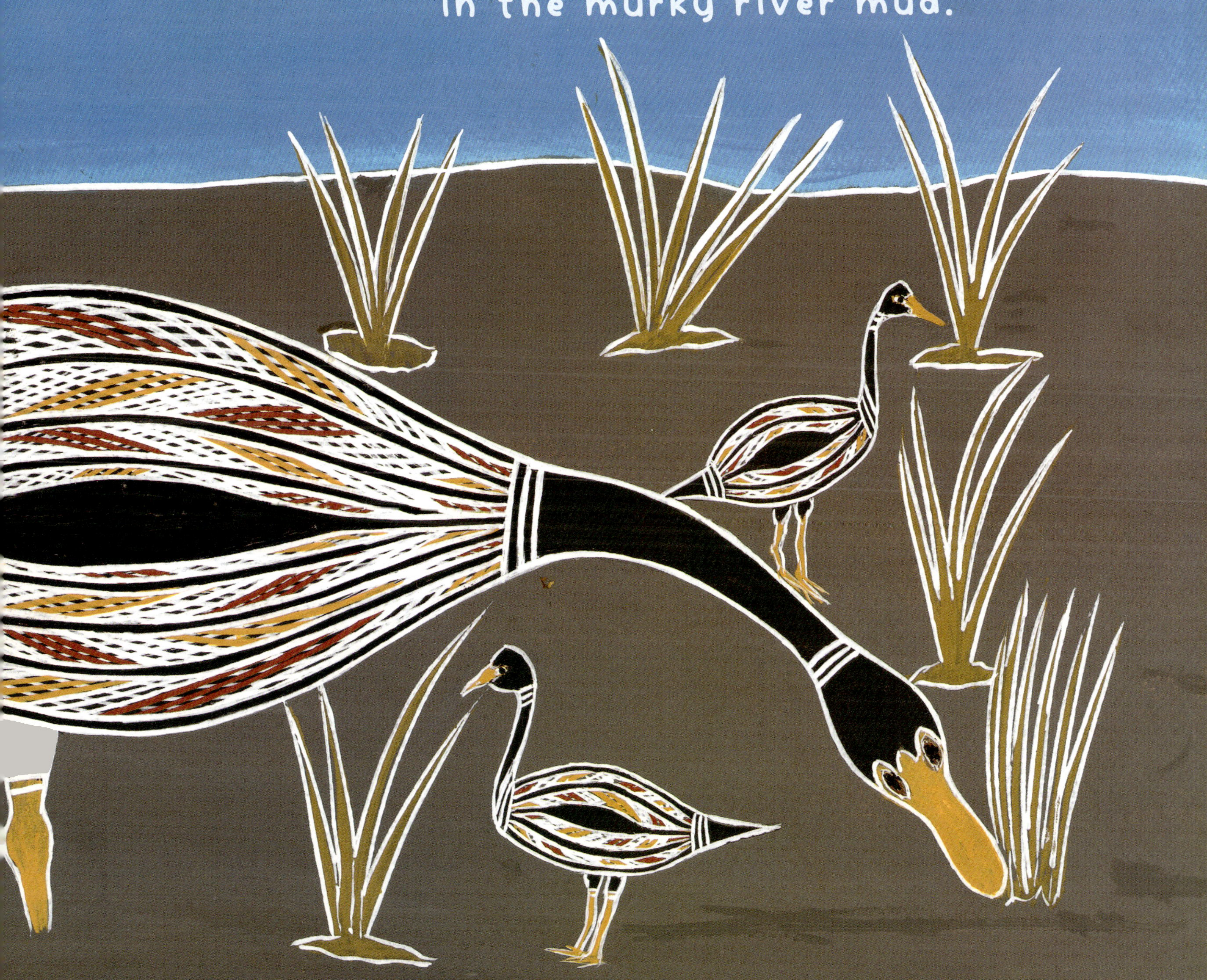

Look with your eyes,

what do you **see**?

I see a **snake**,

SLIDE, SLIDE, SLIDING

among the low river bushes.

Listen with your ears,
what do you **hear**?

I hear a **crocodile**,

CHOMP, CHOMP, CHOMPING

on the muddy river bank.

I love the river near my home.

I look with my eyes,
I listen with my ears,

I learn about the birds and
the animals who love the
river like I do.

And they learn
about me!

Sally Morgan belongs to the Palyku people from the Pilbara, Western Australia. She loves writing stories for children and is excited to once again have such a talented artist as Johnny Warrkatja Malibirr bring her story to life. Sally is the author of the groundbreaking autobiography *My Place.*

Johnny Warrkatja Malibirr is a Yolŋu man from the Ganalbingu clan and is known for his paintings of Ganalbingu song lines as well as his mother's Wägilak clan stories. Along with other members of his clan Johnny keeps culture strong through painting, song, dance and ceremony. He travelled to Canberra in 2000 and performed at the official opening of *Aboriginal Modern Worlds* exhibition at the National Gallery of Australia. Johnny lives in the remote East Arnhem Land community of Gapuwiyak, where he is Chair of the Gapuwiyak Culture and Arts Aboriginal Corporation.

In 2019 Johnny was the winner of Magabala Books' inaugural Kestin Indigenous Illustrator Award, from which he illustrated *Little Bird's Day* the first book he did with author Sally Morgan.

Gapuwiyak Culture and Arts was incorporated in 2007. Owned by its Yolŋu members, the organisation has an all Yolŋu board, and employs a manager and arts workers. The proceeds from sales go to the artists (60%) and contribute to the running of the art centre (40%). It supports more than one hundred artists from Gapuwiyak and surrounding homelands, assisting artists to collect and prepare materials, make high-quality art, explore ideas, develop knowledge and skills, and exhibit, market and sell their work. The centre also runs tourism and cultural programs and is a great place to meet, relax, enjoy a coffee and learn about Yolŋu culture and art. http://gapuwiyak.com.au facebook.com/ Gapuwiyak instagram.com/ gapuwiyakcultureandarts

Also from Sally Morgan and Johnny Warrkatja Malibirr